Stories in a Nutshell

Compiled by

Shreya Pataskar

NOTION PRESS

NOTION PRESS

India. Singapore. Malaysia.

Writers who have contributed to this anthology with their work:

Shreya Pataskar

Rutika Jariwala

Amritha Varshini K.S

Priyanka Banerjee

Saheli Banerji

Ayushi Jain

Nithish Jangili

Abhishek S. Kallolikar

Harika Sattiraju

Shikha Nangru

Kaviya Raghu

Vimal Achintya

Sanjay Ram

Nivetha Chandran

Mohanasrrhee K.M

Munila Naqvi

Shikha Patel

Divit Lokesh Perumalla

Radhakrishnan Santhose Kumar

Stories in a Nutshell

Contents

CONTENTS

About the author

Shreya Pataskar *is a poet and writer hailing from Pune, Maharashtra, India. She began writing as a hobby, but later developed a deeper interest in it. Till date, she has co-authored many anthologies of poems and short stories as well as compiled and published some of them. She writes on WordPress and Instagram. For her, writing is a source to express her ideas and emotions and make her feel free and happy. She believes that words have enough power to change the world*

and that's what she tries to do. She wants to improve and grow as a writer in the future.

Connect with her on Instagram:
@__the.unsaid.words__

War wins, people don't

Of all the important historical events that took place in the past, war between two or more countries has always been the worst. All the bloodshed, decline in the economic status of the respective countries, and most importantly, the feeling of hatred and anger towards the adversaries. The countries would obviously want to win the war, which is why they're ready to sacrifice their own citizens for that. A country might win a war, or for that matter, every war it fights. But can it really be considered as a victory? What do the soldiers who fight a war really think about?

It was 2 a.m.. The night sky was glittering with starts. It was snowing heavily. Under this beautiful sky, the army camps were set up where the soldiers ate and slept, if they were lucky enough to survive. Living away from their families was not the only difficult task for them, but the dilemma of saving their lives or sacrificing them for their country was the worst. How could one make the right choice? But they did that everyday.

"Everybody listen up. We have received orders from the government for covering an area of 25kms more than what we have already covered. The enemy can attack us anytime. Before they attack us, we have to make the first move. We have exactly one hour to move towards the northern borders. Am I clear?"

"Yes sir!" they all replied in synchronization and saluted their chief.

They were loaded with arms and ammunition. Their healthy and strong bodies, along with their sharp minds were ready to fight and win the war. They put off the campfire and sat in their cars to head towards the northern borders. Their jobs didn't allow them to sleep, shiver in the snow, enjoy a hot cup of coffee or eat fresh food everyday. And they didn't allow themselves to feel sad about any of it. They were happily carrying out their duties towards their nation.

They reached the borders and took their positions. They were as alert as a bird. But the enemy was smarter than them. The enemy was already present there, covering themselves by hiding behind the trees and boulders. Bullets were fired one after the another. A few soldiers were injured and a few were martyred.

One of the soldiers who were injured, limped to find shelter. He had used up all the bullets that he had on him. He was barely able to walk. After roaming around for a while, he finally found an underground room. The room had food supplies, medical supplies, guns and bullets. Such rooms were common in the military areas and war zones. In adverse conditions, the soldiers used to sleep in such 'secret rooms'. But that day, the room was empty. The soldier felt relieved after sitting down. He was bleeding heavily from his left leg. He was flinching with pain. His brown colored uniform had turned into red. He managed to clean the blood, medicate his wound and tie a bandage, sighed deeply and lied down.

He didn't even realize when he fell asleep. He woke up startled as he heard footsteps. *'Did the enemy find out about this room? Is this going to be my last day on this planet?'* he thought to himself. He stood up with a rifle And he was right about the footsteps.

One of the soldiers from the opponent's army had entered the room. He was wearing a blue uniform, and he was shot in his right leg. His uniform was torn from a few places. He was startled at the sight of the soldier who was standing with a rifle in his hand. He didn't expect anyone to be present in the room. As a reflex action, he raised his gun too.

"What are you doing here? You're not supposed to be here. Go away before I kill you!" shouted the one with the brown uniform.

"You'll kill me only if I didn't kill you first!" They stood there in silence for a minute, and then the one with the blue uniform lowered his gun.

"Forget it. Just let me rest here for a while, and I'll go away. We don't need to kill each other."

The other soldier lowered his gun. "Fine. You can sleep here if you want to."

"Do you think I am a fool? What if you kill me when I'm asleep?"

"No, I won't kill you."

"Well, I don't want to trust you. You are our enemy."

"We are enemies outside this room. But now, we are just two humans who need rest and medical care. It's snowing out there...." The other soldier calmed down after listening to his words. He looked away.

"Makes sense." They both sat there in silence for a few minutes, until the soldier with the blue uniform tried to start a conversation.

"You must be missing your family, right?"

"Oh, who doesn't?" he sighed in grief. "I'd get to meet them if I survive tonight."

"What do you think? Your country will win this war?"

He started at him in anger, but replied after taking a deep breath. " I don't know!"

"Don't you think its crazy, this whole war thing? I mean, why are wars fought? For money? For power? For resources? Or what?"

"Those are some of the reasons behind fighting wars..."

"Wars are fought because the human race is dumb! We indicate national borders on the land as well as on maps. But the truth is, these borders exist in our minds."

"Well, there won't be any countries as such, if there are no borders!"

"That's exactly my point! What do these borders make us do? Hate and kill humans who are just like us. It appears like one country benefits and the other loses at the end. But it isn't like that."

"I agree. Humans are so greedy that their thoughts are clouded with greed, due to which they cannot think before making cruel decisions. Politics is important than human lives, be it anywhere on this planet!"

"The leaders care only about how much goes inside their pockets! As if they're going to take their money and their political power to their graves."

"Just imagine how the world would have been if there were no national borders. Just acres and acres of land, all belonging to the humans. No barriers. No wars. No bloodshed!"

"Sadly, this will be just a dream, a dream of the Utopian world! We think the country which we're fighting with is our enemy. But the real enemy is greed."

"That's right. Greed is the worst enemy of humans. But look how unfortunate we are!

Just because they're greedy, we have to pay the price of our lives, by giving up on all the joys that life has to offer. We sacrifice our lives for our country, which is what the narrative is."

"Yeah, we actually sacrifice our lives so that the common man gets to live a happy life, which isn't entirely false. But ultimately, our leaders sleep peacefully as they find their way to benefit from the war. By the time one war ends, they're ready with the agenda for the next one. Who cares about us? Which leader genuinely cares for their country?"

"Right. Countries are made and run by the people living in it. If the leaders really cared about their 'countries', the first and the most important task would have been to protect the people of their country, including us."

"I totally agree with you. They think that they win, as leaders or as the representatives of the respective country, but they're the ones who lose badly."

"I hope that some day, maybe after a 100 years, the leaders realize that every time their country fights a war against the other, its the war who wins, and not any of the countries. People die. People suffer a lot. But they don't win. Only the 'war' wins!"

They both felt a good connection with each other. They dozed off besides each other. At sunrise, they both helped each other get up and walked out of the room with hands on each other's shoulders. Their battalions had already returned to their destinations; and it didn't bother these soldiers. They weren't even curious about which country had won the war. They were just glad to erase the 'borders' in their minds.

That day, war, along with friendship, became victorious.

About the author

Rutika Jariwala *is from Surat, Gujarat. By profession, she is a dental student, a bit chubby and lazy. Her escape is writing poetry and stories. She still goes to sleep hearing mamma's lories. Probably, in future, you might find her fixing your tooth and she narrating to you her poetries.*

Connect with her on Instagram:
@the_poetry_hub

Story of the three dogs

There were three dogs. Three of them had different qualities.

Max: He was a brave dog.

Charlie: He was an intelligent dog.

Cooper: He was an innocent dog.

One early morning, Cooper went in search for food and there he was surrounded by other dogs of the city. It was quite a long time they surrounded him but didn't do anything. Max and Charlie realized that it's been a long time and he hasn't come back. They came out and started searching him. Charlie found Cooper and started barking at other dogs. Max came and saw that Cooper was in danger, and he started running towards the other dogs and while fighting with them, he got injured. Charlie and Cooper came near him and took him home.

Let me tell you a small story of mine life:

One day, when I was in high school, there was a girl who was walking around in the school. She never used to talk with anyone neither did she care about what's happening in the school. She always used to be in her own world. Her name was Olivia. One day, I thought of talking to her, but she ignored me! On the next day, I tried to talk to her again, but she ignored. On that day, I went home and thought about her the whole day and ended with a conclusion that whatever happens I will try my best to talk with her.

On the third day, again I went to her and asked her that why she always stays alone. She replied, "Children over here don't like me." and she ran.

My heart went out for her. I ran behind her and saw tears in her eyes. As I as went towards her, she told me everything about her what happened with her since day one of the school. And then I decided to help her out and make her feel that she is not alone and I am with her. She smiled at me. That smile was of real gratitude. I asked her for lunch at my place and after school, we went home together. We talked all the way long and we shared a lot of things with each other. After lunch, I asked her to join me with my friends to play badminton. She said yes.

Gradually, we became good friends. The more I got to know about Olivia, the more I liked her. She was a pure soul. We used to hanged out on weekends and used to spend a lot of time together. As the time passed, everyone in the school started talking with her and never made her feel that she is alone. Till today we are best friends and we share the same bond which we used to share in our high school. Till today we share everything with each-other even if it's worst or good. We always stand together in our good & bad times.

Moral of the story: Always remember that those who are with you in your difficult times are the ones who really love you and care for you.

About the author:

Amirtha Varshini K.S *is a high school student. She was born in April 10 2005. She has always been fascinated with stories since she was a child. She began writing in a young age and has used it is a medium of expressing her emotions. She is also passionate about cooking and considers herself a foodie. She is always looking for new experiences to engage in.*

Connect with her on Instagram :
*@random_writings_of_mine_*

The delayed death of Mrs. Ira Payne

It was supposed to be quick, like every other innocent victims of mine. I hated watching their family suffer. Especially, the little girl Naomi, daughter of my next victim. She did not deserve to live without her mother, Ira Payne.

Ira was giving birth to her second child. This time, a son. She was supposed to die as soon as she gives birth so that her family didn't have to go through the pain of watching her struggle and suffer. But that did not happen, Why, you ask? Well, I am late. Without me, she can't die. I was running late for my job, just because I was not able to find my black hooded robe.

I could sense that by now Ira had given birth, but was in a critical condition, Her soul hanging on to her body by a string. I was supposed to be there to cut the string loose. I could see that the doctors were giving hope to the husband, who was holding Naomi tightly. The baby boy was safe, under medical supervision. I had to hurry up and end all their sufferings.

On some days, I hated my job. Today is one of those days. I hated killing innocent people, but I had to. I had to maintain the balance. On some days, I enjoy my job. I enjoy killing those worthless evil people. How can a man even think about raping a girl? How cruel and twisted is he? I enjoyed killing rapists, letting their death be the longest, making them go through as much pain as possible. My job was not easy. People assumed so many things about me. Some think I am just a feeling. Some think that I am darkness. But in reality, I was just an immortal person with too much power and some big responsibility. I am death. Death is me.

As soon as I found my robes, I put them on and I rushed to the hospital. I stood there in the room, invisible to everyone but Ira.

"Are you here to..." Ira asked, unable to finish her sentence. No one else in the room could see or hear this interaction. To them, everything seemed normal.

"Yes, Ira. It's time for you to go" I said trying to make it easy for her. Ira stared at me. All of me. Everything from the long black hair to the black sandals I was wearing.

"You are a woman, aren't you? Then you should understand that I have to stay. I have to stay here for my children. I just had a baby. My husband will not be able to raise them without me. Please let me live!" She begged me.

People always assumed that if I, death, was a person, it would be a man. Oh, how they are wrong! A lot of people find it surprising that I am a woman.

"Ira, Please don't make it harder than it has to be, It is your, fate." I told her trying to make it easier for her. Ira was sobbing.

"Death...Or whatever your name is, I understand, I do. But can you please do me one last favor. Please? Can you make that my family knows I love them unconditionally! Tell Naomi, Mommy will be always with her, watching over her and lastly tell my husband the name our son Issac, after my father." Ira asked me. I could sense that she was ready, ready to leave.

"I will try my best Ira," I said and cut her string, The string which kept her soul to her body. I was not going to delay her death any longer.

I looked around the room. I could see her heart monitor go flat. The husband stared at it. He did not need the doctors to tell him. He knew his wife was gone...forever. I wanted to fulfill Ira's favor. That's the least I could do. I prolonged her death, I made her family suffer. So I went near the husband. I was still invisible to them. And I passed on Ira's message to him. He would have not heard my voice, rather he would have heard Ira and had a strong emotion that his wife would have wanted to name their son Issac. Now, he knew that his wife loved him deeply.

Next, I went to Naomi. I would pass on her message a little differently. Today in her dream, She would dream of mommy, she would understand how much mommy loved her and how mommy will always be with her. I smiled looking at the little girl. She had such loving parents.

Next, even though Ira didn't ask me to, I went to the baby boy Issac. I made sure that as he grows, he will be surrounded by love, knowing his mother loved him. I also promised myself I would not kill him until he has lived a nice and long life.

As soon as I was done with fulfilling Ira's favor. I fled the place. That family would have a happy life, but it was time for me to move on, I have to choose my next victim, this time it will be someone horrible, so I don't feel guilty doing my job. I had to live my life as death....forever.

About the author:

Priyanka Banerjee *is an avid reader and an amateur writer. She is from West Bengal, India. She was a student of a vernacular school and was always passionate about teaching. She is an M.A in English and also completed her B.Ed. From her childhood she used to scribble a lot. Gradually, all the scribbling turned into writings. She loves to write her heart out. Now, she is a teacher of an English medium school. Besides being a teacher and a writer, she is also an explorer . She writes short stories, poems, micro tales and open letters and travel diaries. Many of her write-ups have already been published.*

Connect with her on Instagram: @pprbanerjee7

A Quest for Heaven

Yasi was sitting outside of her house and she was staring at the hill which was not far from her house. She had heard from Kamala aunty that some children like her lived there. Yasi was thinking about the good old days when her grandfather took her for an evening walk. Though that was not a perfect 'walk' for her, but her grandfather used to say "Yasi, let's have a walk together."

Sitting alone on her wheel chair, Yasi was recollecting those stories which her grandfather used to tell her. Yasi never saw her grandmother as she passed away before Yasi's birth, but her grandfather used to tell so many stories about his beloved wife that Yasi could visualize everything.

Yasi's reverie broke by the voice of Kamala aunty. In the soft twilight, Yasi saw that all the birds were going back to their nests. Every evening when she saw this, she knew this was her time also to go to her room. Sighing, Yasi turned her wheel chair. Every time she looked at the sky, a question came to her mind- 'Is there really a beautiful heaven beyond the sky?'

Yasi was a girl of twenty-two. Her father was a well-known businessman. Yasi got everything she needed, but somehow she was not happy from within. Her grandfather was her only friend in her family whom she had lost four years ago. Now, there was no one to tell her stories or to take her for a walk in the evening.

Yasi herself roamed here and there near her house. Kamala aunty was her only friend after the demise of her grandfather. Since childhood, Yasi knew that she was different from her elder sister, Malini. Every time, on every occasion, she understood that Malini got more importance than her. Later, she understood that the only difference between Malini and her was that Malini did not have to use a wheelchair to go here and there.

Yasi's family never felt the importance of spending as much money for Yasi as they spent for Malini's education. Malini used to go to a well-known school, whereas Yasi was sent to another school where the school fees were less than half of Malini's school fees.

Yasi never complained or wept for all these

Negligence. Rather, she thought that all this is quite natural as she was habituated with these since her childhood.

The day when Malini went to London for her higher studies, she saw that her father was bragging before one of their neighbours.

" Yes, Mr. Roy, Malini is my quotable daughter . Let my daughter complete her M.B.A, then she will take the oar of my business."

Yasi never heard this phrase-'my daughter' from her father for her. It was Yasi's twenty third birthday. She knew except Kamala aunty, no one was there to wish her. Yasi had a hidden wish for a long time and the urge of fulfilling her wish was increasing day by day.

Yasi was lying on the bed when Kamala aunty entered into her room with a big smile " Happy birthday Yasi, wake up quickly! Today, I will take you to the foot of that hill. There is a temple. Do you want to go there? It's been long you did not go for a walk, let's go today."

After four long years, Yasi again heard someone who offered her 'a walk' just as her grandfather did.

Yasi nodded and said, "Aunty I have a request."

Kamala aunty was looking at her questioningly. "I want to go on the other side of the hill."

Yasi kept on saying "I want to meet all those who are like me."

Kamala aunty agreed. It was 10a.m when Yasi reached the orphanage. There were many children. Some were physically challenged and some were not. Yasi found six children who used wheel chair like her. Yasi was amazed to see that there was no discrimination among those children. All were playing together, no one was neglected. Everyone was being treated equally. Everyone was happy there.

This was something which was beyond her imagination. This was the first time when she started to think herself as equal to the other members of her family. She spent a good time there. She told the children some stories of kings and queens which was told to her by her grandfather. She also had her lunch with them – this was the first time she was having lunch so happily as she never got a chance to sit with her family members during lunch or dinner time.

In the evening, she returned home. This was the first time she did not feel abandoned. This was the first time she felt as normal as the other people. This was the first time when she found a place where she got the treatment like a family member. Somehow, she felt a strong connection with those children of that orphanage. Their innocent smiles were floating in front of her eyes. She began going to the orphanage regularly and spent a good amount of time there. Gradually, she started to go there without the help of Kamala aunty and spent more and more time with those children. The other members of the orphanage liked Yasi very much.

Days passed. It had been almost a year Yasi was working in the orphanage as a teacher. She stayed there with the other members of the orphanage and rarely went home to meet her parents. Kamala aunty often came to the orphanage to see Yasi.

Yasi was twenty four. This year the whole orphanage celebrated Yasi's birthday with splendour. Of course, Kamala aunty was present there, after all it was Kamala aunty who first brought Yasi into her heaven.

About the author:

Saheli Banerji is from Kolkata, West Bengal. Although she is a former Lecturer of English, but writing has always been her passion and presently she has opted for it as her profession too! Along with being a poet and short stories writer, she is a professional novelist too.

You can find my works

1. Pools of Blood

2. Murder of the king

3. Miscellany of odes

4. Rhythms of Life

5. Zingedi ek Eheshas

For more information you can find me on Google. Just type my name!

Connect with her on Instagram: @saheli_gobu

The last promise

Once upon a time in a faraway land,- no, no. I can't begin this story like this. This is neither a fairy tale nor a tale of pirates and dragons. I don't want the traditional laid back cliché attached to this. This is a story of two friends. Two friends whose lives revolved around each other. They were like two stars in a galaxy joined by a delicate thread of love.

Ajay and Prabhakar met in an unexpected way. One night there was a heavy downpour. Ajay, a young bespectacled lean boy of sixteen, went to the market to buy fritters. "Bhajiyas" or "bhajjis" as we call in Hindi. They are deep fried potatoes in a batter of gram flour, and are served with " pudiney ki chatney" and tea, an ambrosiac for Indians during rains. Mmm.. My mouth is salivating simply by the thought of it. No. I can't get distracted. So where was I? Yes. Ajay was standing under his umbrella waiting for his turn to buy "bhajjis". Suddenly someone ran up from behind. Snatched the umbrella and started whacking a man with it. Ajay was startled. He turned around to see a boy of his age was whacking a man with his umbrella, swearing words which would make one's ears fall off. The man was trying his best to escape, but the boy had a tight grip. Just like we dust off dirt from our clothes with a duster, the boy was literally dusting the man with the umbrella. Ajay was spellbound.

'Who was he? Why was he beating the shit out of the man?', he wondered. Slowly a crowd started to form. A few burly men came up and tried to stop the boy.

'Please leave him. He is already half dead. Just let him go..', they tried to pull him back. Ajay's umbrella was already in pieces. At last the man got a chance of escaping and he disappeared in the rain. The boy was still fuming in anger. He went and sat down on a bench of the fry shop. Ajay went up to him and before he could demand a compensation for breaking his umbrella, the boy spoke out, 'I am sorry for breaking your umbrella like

that. I was angry and I didn't realize what I was   doing.'
'What had happened actually? Who was that man? Why were you beating him?'

'He sells bidis.'

'What? A tobacconist?'

'Yes.'
Ajay couldn't understand why the boy was beating a bidi seller all of a sudden. That's weird!
'So, why were you determined to turn him into a pulp?'
'He deserved that. I had ordered him some packets of Sutra Bidi, premium quality. He promised me that he would deliver them today. But from morning his shop is closed. I have been searching him throughout the day. Suddenly I saw him here buying bhajjis. I ran up, took your umbrella and bang!'

Ajay starred at him in disbelief. For a packet of bidis, who does that? What a strange boy!

'Its not for a packet of bidis', the boy uttered. He seemed to read Ajay's mind. ' He broke

his promise. That's what made me angry. He could have apologized. But he simply tried to flee. I hate people who break promises'.
'Promises are made to be broken, my dear.'

'No. not for me. If we go against our own words, we are not better than animals, are we?'

His eyes were shining under the street lights. He had a character which is rarely found among people. He was brave, straightforward and honest. Ajay instantly liked him. 'I am Ajay'.

'Prabhakar'.

And then it began. Their friendship. Life became an adventure for them. Seeing them together people used to idolize them as ' Jay and Biru of Sholay'. Prabhakar was a tall, well built boy with curly hair and a pointed nose and sharp eyes. Ajay on the other hand, was a meek lamb in specs.

Years passed like this. They graduated from college. Prabhakar was to shift to USA for higher studies. Ajay was to join a software company at Hyderabad. On the day of convocation, they went back to the bhajiya shop for the last time. Everything was just the way it was before. Nothing had changed; the shop, the yummy fries, the heavenly smell and the benches, except the fact that they had grown older.

'I would be leaving for States in a few days', Prabhakar said, munching the fritters.'

'I know. I am gonna miss you. But I am happy for you. Its always been your dream to do your research from US.

'Gonna miss you too. Miss this place. Miss these fries. And our college canteen'.

'You are saying as if you are never gonna come back. You are going to forget me, are you?'

"That's never gonna happen. No matter, where I be, you will always be the last man I would visit before I leave earth.

'Promise?'

'Yeah. Promise'.

That was the last time they met. Although, they regularly kept in touch, contacted each other, but Ajay and Prabhakar couldn't end up meeting. Even when Ajay got married, Prabhakar attended his wedding by raising a glass of champagne to the web cam. When Prabhakar met Rita, an Indian based biologist, working at his lab, he introduced her to his best buddy on video. No matter how busy they were, they always ended up calling each other and sharing their lives.

Then one day, something happened and life never became the same for two. It was raining hard. Just like the night they met. Lightening flashed the sky. A cyclone was brewing .The whole ambience looked like a monster trying to gulp down the city all at once. There was a turmoil inside Ajay's house too. His wife had filed for divorce that morning. She was tired of staying with a man who can't provide her children. Was it Ajay's fault? He wasn't sexually impotent. The doctors had recommended some therapies. But his wife had lost patience and she wanted to be free. Ajay was tired and broken. He had always been a good husband but the result of his goodness came in the form of a seven word letter. He had already finished a bottle of whiskey when Prabhakar called. 'Hey mate! You okay?'

'Yeah. Just a bit drunk. How is Rita doing? I heard the delivery date is on due'.

'She is at hospital. They called. It's a boy! Can you imagine? I m a father now. And you are uncle'.

'Oh really! I am so happy! So where are you now?'

'I am driving. I have brought some flowers for her. On my way to see my champ'.

Ajay didn't want to spoil Prabhakar's mood. 'That dude is happy. I don't want him to worry about me now'.

'Do you remember that bhajjiwala?'

'Yeah. I still miss those fries,dude'.

'Do you remember how we promised each other that we would meet again and have bhajji and wine?'

'Yeah. How can I forget? I wish you were here, blessing my child. '

'Yeah. I wish'.

The line suddenly got disconnected. Maybe network problem. Ajay opened another bottle. He wanted to drown himself by drinking. He was so immersed in grief, so lonely. Outside wind was roaring like a tiger in a cage. Suddenly, there was a knock on the door. Ajay was already half asleep. Stumbling and tottering, he groped for the switches. There was no currant. Electricity had long gone home. Switching on his mobile flash, he went downstairs and opened the door. There stood a tall man with curly hair, completely drenched in rain, grinning wildly. 'Prabhakar!'

'Yey pal!', he shouted in happiness and hugged Ajay tightly.

'Prabhu! My buddy! You are really here?', Ajay cried in joy. He ushered his long lost friend inside the house and gave him a towel to dry. Ajay was so drunk that he didn't realize how would Prabhakar appear there all of a sudden. He was too much euphoric to see his friend after such a long time.

'You know, I always keep my promise. I had to come to see you. I was missing you Prabhu. Its been such along time'.

'Ajay. Why don't you arrange a bottle of wine and some bhajjiya, just like old times sake?'

'Sure. Come on'.

For Ajay, it was a memorable time. In the midst of his grief, Prabhakar came as silver lining. He opened his heart before him, poured out all his pain and miseries. Prabhakar was a good listener. He consoled Ajay and urged him to move on.

'Ajay. You have a long journey ahead. You cant drown yourself in grief anymore. Let bygones be bygones. Promise me, you are not going to drink from now on. Promise me you will be a strong man'.
Ajay nodded. Prabhakar led him to his bedroom and tucked him in. For the first time after many years Ajay felt peace.
'Ajay?'
'Hmm?'
'If anything happens to me, promise me, you will take care of my son'.
'Yeah. Why not? But don't worry, nothing would happen to you.' Prabhakar smiled.
Slowly, Ajay fell asleep.

A loud blaring noise woke him up. The phone had been ringing for a long time. His head was reeling and his eyes were still heavy with sleep.

'Hello?'

'Hello Ajay?' Some one was sobbing from the other end. He woke up in an instant.
'Its Rita here'.
'Hey Rita. Why are you crying? How is the baby?'
'Baby is fine. There is a bad news.' She sobbed.
'What happened?'
'Yesterday afternoon, Prabhakar was on his way to the hospital. Suddenly a truck came from wrong side and hit the car. The car rolled over and got smashed. Prabhakar--'
She couldn't continue anymore. She broke down into tears. Ajay's blood ran cold. He looked at the table. A few pieces of bhajjiyas were still there. The phone clattered on the floor and everything blacked out.

About the author

*22 year old **Ayushi Jain** is a BMM graduate and aspires to become a writer. She believes that words can create magic and make people smile. Apart from weaving words, she loves to paint and hog on food joints in her free time.*

*Connect with her on Instagram: @_aayushi_jain_*

An inseparable love

It was a dark and stormy morning. The streets were empty, trees uprooted, and it rained heavily. People shut themselves in their houses to avoid the chilly wind. A 16-year-old girl stood near the window. She watched the gust of wind blowing away the notes, the cap, and all the things that laid on the empty streets. Some people wanted to go out and experience the weather. While some just wanted to cuddle in their cosy blankets.

Two hours later, the wind stopped blowing. The streets were calm and lifeless until people started stepping outside their house. A group of children jumped and danced in one corner. Another group of teenagers played gully cricket. Some felt crappy because of the weather. While some enjoyed the little haze.

But, in this midst of chaos, there was Saurabh. He was in his room, sitting in one corner, distressed and unsettled. His eyes looked terrified.

Knock Knock!

Saurabh sat there, disturbed, and ignored the continuous knocks on his door. After a few seconds, his maid entered the room. She wore a light blue midi with a white apron on it. Her short and curly brown hair complemented her black eyes. She held a tray with a glass of milk and two *parathas* in it.

'Saurabh baba, please get up and have your breakfast,' said the maid.

Saurabh nodded and rubbed his hands on his face. He got up and sat on his bed. His messed up clothes made him look shabby.

'Keep the breakfast here. I'll eat it later,' said Saurabh while covering himself in a blanket.

The maid kept the breakfast tray on the bedside table and left. Saurabh tried to sleep, but couldn't. His eyes were locked on the door until a strange smile appeared on his face.

'You came early today,' said Saurabh.

'Look at you, Saurabh. Why are you doing this to yourself?' asks Trisha.

Saurabh exhaled and ignored her

question. Trisha took the chair near the window and sat on it. She tied her long and silky black hair that made her look more elegant. She took a deep breath and looked at Saurabh. Shedding tears of grief, she broke the silence.

'Quitting all the things that make you happy won't heal you,' said Trisha rubbing her nose.

'Maybe life would have been the same if you never left.'

'Life is unpredictable, you know. We don't have any control over it.'

'It was my fault. I shouldn't have done it.'

'No, it wasn't. Stop blaming yourself for everything.'

'Trisha, I wake up every day in the hope that all of this is just a nightmare. It will all be normal again. We will sit in the drawing room, watch our favourite movies, and laugh uncontrollably. But, I know, life is never going to be the same.'

'I know things have been very rough lately. But, you need to give life one more chance.'

Trisha stood up and caressed Saurabh's hair. She was about to leave when Saurabh held her hand and started sobbing.

'Please don't go. It's getting difficult each passing day,' shouted Saurabh.

'I will have to leave. I can't be here forever. You have to start living for yourself again. And remember, we are inseparable. No matter what, we will be together, always. Nothing will make me happier than seeing the old you again.,' said Trisha and disappeared.

'Please come back!' yelled Saurabh.

He cried continuously until the maid entered his room.

'Saurabh baba, whom were you talking to?'

'It was Trisha. She was just here, talking to me.'

'No, she wasn't. You need to take your medicines and have some sleep.'

With tears in his eyes, Saurabh laid on his bed and remembered the tragic accident that took Trisha's life. A year ago, Saurabh and Trisha went to their terrace to enjoy the spectacular view of the sunset. They sat on the roof of the terrace and talked about their dreams and fantasies. After a while, they started mocking each other. But, at one point, Saurabh hit her hard, just for fun, because of which Trisha lost her balance and fell down. She was Saurabh's younger sister, and her accident had left him shaken. The grieving process only made him see her through hallucinations and have conversations with her. Till today, he blames himself for her death. As days passed by, his guilt only increased. No matter how hard he tried, he never had the courage to get up and make things right again. Because, when he lost Trisha, he lost a piece of his heart. He lost the will to live.

But despite everything, he continued to love her. He continued to dream about meeting her in another life. And, he continued to smile on every memory they shared together. No wonder, they were and are still inseparable.

About the author:

Nithish Jangili's *dream is to become a film director, a dream since he was in 8th std. Till 8th standard, he changed his dreams many times. But after that, then it was always the same. He writes stories for his short films and movies. He started writing and then fell in love with it. He loves to tell stories to people. He is neither an author nor he dreamt to be one. He writes stories but not like an author. He doesn't know the style of writing, so he wants to become a good storyteller.*

Connect with him on Instagram: @nithish_1507

Love story of an introvert

Sometimes we just want someone to just listen to our story. I just want to share my story with you.

I am a person who....I think the word 'introvert' will be suitable for describing me. I'm the person who is not good at studies and doesn't even have any talents. I don't know how to handle the situations, how to deal with emotions.I don't know how to even talk to people. Maybe that's why I don't have many friends; just a few and those few are just friends, not the best ones. I was confident when my mother was with me. But now, her absence has made me under confident. It makes me fear everything.

I had a girlfriend. She was the one who proposed me. Maybe, she was someone who liked simple people like me. I accepted her proposal because I was surprised that someone liked me and yes, I was in a relationship. Maybe I don't even know how a relationship should be, that's why she broke up with me, just because I was being myself. Someone likes simple but simple gets boring easily. I think that's what happened in my situation. That made me more under confident. I was alone, I was a question mark to myself. From then, I always thought nobody is going to like me. But then, on my birthday, a girl called me. She was my schoolmate. In school, I used to talk to her and after these many years she had remembered my birthday and called me. I was surprised, at that time I didn't know that she is going to be the most important person in my life.

After my birthday, she used to call me regularly text me every day. I used to start my day with her good morning. But why is she doing all that? I always had that question in my mind but I never wanted to know the answer. I liked it that someone cares about me. It makes me feel happy.

She made me break my silence and I started talking to her. I never thought that I can talk like that. Days passed and we became good friends. There was no limit to our conversations. We never felt that we are running out of topics. Sometimes, we even skipped our sleep just to talk. We used to share everything. She used to share everything, even the girl things. She became a habit to me and eventually, I was addicted to her.

I felt happy with her. I felt confident. I had no fear and I just felt like I'm complete when I'm with her. I just wanted someone like her in my life because she was my only friend. She knew me very well. She understood me and supported me. She used to scold me, make me feel confident and taught me everything that I didn't know. I loved to be her friend. I loved her company. I loved her caring and supporting nature. Maybe, I loved her and I decided that I want to be with her for my whole life. I used to feel like I have everything because she was with me.

But, after 6 years of our friendship, she left me. She got married. She left me! She left me in pain. She left me in aggression and in emptiness. I began to question myself again. I was just stuck in a blank space. Why did she did this to me? Did I misunderstood her? Is it my mistake to love a person who doesn't love me? Someone who couldn't understand me loved me, but someone who knows me more than I do, doesn't love me? Why?

There is no answer to any of my questions. The person I loved the most was not with me anymore. She taught me everything but she never taught me how to live without her. I cried and cried and cried for days, for weeks, and even for months.

But then finally I realized that she taught me to live my life. I started moving on but her absence always used to hurt me. When she was with me, I told her everything. But now, I have no one to share my feelings with.

Sometimes we just need someone to listen our pain, our feelings. I have no one to talk to, so I told you my story. I just feel better now, maybe somewhat better. Once I didn't even know how to talk and today I told you my story and this is also because of her.

About the author

Abhishek S.Kallolikar is from Belgaum, Karnataka. He is pursuing B.Tech in Bangalore. He likes riding bike, reading books, listening to music and travelling. Writing is his hobby and a source to share his thoughts, ideas and knowledge with everyone. He says,' My dear reader, like , how the nature has a power to influence the human society, even words have the same power.'

Connect with him on Instagram:

@abhishekskallolikar

Too much care is worse than being careless

College students are always eager to hear about vacations. And My institution had fulfilled this wish of ours. I came home and packed all the essential things. My Destination was Puttur, a town in Karnataka. This town is well known for its culture and beautiful temples. I was accompanied by two of my friends. After reaching Puttur, we freshened up and visited a rich and beautiful temple. In India, it is common to see beggars begging at the entrance of any temple.

There were five beggars and one person was aged above 60. I started a conversation with him instead of giving him a penny. I said 'Namaste' to him and he reciprocated in the same manner. Without my permission, he started telling about his past and the Reason behind his present condition.

He began, "Sir, Myself Byregouda. I am native of this Town itself. I was living with my wife and my Son. We both were uneducated and I wanted my son to study hard and be a good example for our future generations. I worked without taking rest to earn more and more money. At the same time, I was spending money by planning the expenses carefully. I used to always think about my son's education. My son valued every penny I had spent on him. He wanted to become a doctor and worked hard to achieve his goal everyday. I and my wife were glad to see his scores. He completed his primary education and PU here itself. For M.B.B.S, he went to Delhi and I had a tough task to manage the expenses for it. We both slept hungry but made sure that our son would eat till he is full, so that he would be able to study effectively. Till he completed his PG in Delhi, I felt empty. I missed him a lot.

Meanwhile, he completed studies and came to Puttur to meet us. This was a day for us on which we saw sunrise. We all celebrated and enjoyed the moment by eating delicious food and having long conversations. He stayed for 12 days with us. Finally, it was time for him to go back to Delhi for his medical practice. For us, it was a sad moment, but there was no other option.

During his initial days of service, he Used to send us hard cash and we dealt with our daily needs. This continued for a year. But after that, we stopped receiving cash. We were concerned about our son and not on the money. I thought he might have some financial problem. This continued for two years and my heart started aching at the thought of him.

I asked his friend and he told me, "Uncle, your son was involved in unlawful and illegal activities. So, he is behind the bars now."

After hearing this, I was shocked. My feet turned cold and I could feel my heart break into pieces. With tears in my eyes, I narrated the harsh reality of him to my wife. She cried after listening to everything. She was deeply shocked. After some days, she died.

I was falling short of money. I didn't understand what to do. That condition made me take this step. Now, I realize that ethics are more vital than just education. I had cared for our son so much, but he didn't realize it. He might not have thought about the efforts that I took for his studies. Maybe, caring too much for him was my mistake." After listening to this, my tears had no boundary. Even my friends were feeling the same. Then, the three of us entered the temple, took the blessings and we gave

Prasadam to that person and he said 'Have a bright future'.

About the author:

Harika Sattiraju *is an engineer by profession, but a writer at heart. She is very passionate about writing and it is the first thing that she thinks of every morning and the last thing that lulls her to sleep every night. She wants to see herself as an accomplished writer.*

Connect with her on Instagram:

@thewriterscloud_hs

The entwined lives

On a rainy night, when ear splitting thunders accompanied by eye shattering lightnings broke out, Tara shuddered from her deep slumber. On her right was her husband Ranjit tilting his head to his right, disturbed with the way Tara shook in her sleep. The noises in the silent night reverberated, making it hard for Tara to fall asleep as the increased decibels of sound echoed in the silent night.

As a matter of habit, she pulled her phone and kept rummaging through random apps and several social networking sites. Seeing her online, one of her colleagues messaged her.

'Look! Who is online today! It's shocking but I'm happy.'

As an instinctive action, she replied with a smiley, half occupied with the breath taking scene she witnessed outside her window. As if suddenly pulling her from a beautiful reverie, the light in her bedroom was switched on. Her heart skipped a beat, as she saw her husband standing right at her back. His eyes were filled with unspoken anger. Half sleepy and half angry, he was looking ghostly with the gloomy environment all around making the scene more gruesome.

"To whom were you messaging at this odd hour? It's half past twelve." he pressed each syllable even though it was not needed.

Tara was shocked. 'He doesn't trust me.' This thought was piercing her more than maybe a hundred needles altogether. Her heavy heart was about to explode through her eyes, but her mind was so adamant to give away.

'Now is not the time to either succumb or fight. I need to handle it well.' she thought.

"Ranjit, you know me just for few days. So, you may have misunderstood me. As a working woman, I interact with many men all through the day." She continued, pausing for a minute to see what effect her words were having on him. He seemed quite in thought and the insecurity slightly leaving his eyes.

"I was not messaging anyone, just dropped a smiley to a male friend of mine who had messaged. I will talk with him tomorrow as it's an odd hour." These words were spoken with a slight increase in the voice's tone to have an effect that she too realized that it was late.

"You may have the doubt that why did I send a smiley today. That I too cannot answer. Maybe a habit of talking with friends irrespective of gender."

He looked into her eyes even for more than few silent minutes, and continued.

"Sorry Tara, I was a bit judgemental."

"It's okay Ranjit. I am happy that I could not only clarify the matter but also I am sure I made myself clear. I don't take you wrong even if you speak with women and same is the case with me."

Ranjit's face was flushed with guilt having asked his newly wed wife such a question as he thought of himself as a progressive man. Out of many things, a marriage teaches people, who are bound in such a beautiful bond, are respect and trust. It is not a one way process but a two way road and the most essential qualities of any relationship.

Ranjit wound his left hand around Tara's waist as Tara rested her head on his shoulder. They both kept glancing into the dark starless night as the outpouring outside continued.

About the author

Shikha Nangru *is a content writer and has been working professionally for the last 2 years. Hailing from the capital city of India, Shikha loves to travel and observe human relationships. She would love to redefine feminism and delightfully calls herself a feminist writer.*

Having pursued her education in literature, she often finds herself entangled in the world of stories. When the feminist writer is not lost in one of her own creations, she is found whiling away the hours reading novels & scripts, or watching content-driven movies and web shows. She is a reader by the day and a writer by the night.

A singer by heart, a makeup artist by certification and a writer by profession, Shikha Nangru calls herself a crazy ball locked up in an empty birdcage.

To get a glimpse into her life, check out her Instagram @shikhanangru.

To get in touch with her, shoot a mail at shikhanangru@gmail.com.

The silent prick

Hardly daring to breathe, Anika struggled to lift herself. Attempting to shoot her left leg in the air, Anika managed to grab hold of the blanket before she opened her eyes. At once, she sat up in horror gasping for breath. Raising the beaded brow, she looked up and observed the silence in the room as the ghosts of her dream vanished into thin air. Anika was still hyperventilating as she poured a glass of water, peeking outside the window with a watchful eye.

Purrs from outside the glass window pierced through the silence of the night. She had named the stray Mrs. Norris, borrowing from her favourite series of novels. As she opened the shutter of the glass window, Mrs. Norris jumped onto the floor ambling through the room gazing at every corner searching for her bowl of milk. Ineffective in her search, Mrs. Norris turned towards Anika and purred again. Picking up her newest baby, Anika went to the kitchen. The stream of milk was disturbed by Mrs. Norris's silent banter. No sooner the milk was poured than the baby kitten was served with her dinner.

As Anika decided to clean the spilled milk from the top of her kitchen shelf, her mother's words echoed in her ears.

"Inu you'll have to stop responding to them in anger." she continued, "What would I do if they harmed you outside school?"

"But mom they touched my...." Anika paused reluctantly as her mother interrupted.

"Then complain to your ma'am." the mother asserted, "I want you to come back home safely sweety".

Anika remembered how the two boys were suspended from the school as she had expressed her grievances to her school teacher. The very thought comforted her in times of distress. The 16-year old was instructed not to fight the boys in her school. However, the mother did teach her daughter to raise her voice against them. It was for the law to take the rightful action. It was time, she realized to arm the women of the society against their perpetrators. Without stopping to think, she grabbed her phone from her room and dialed a number.

"I'm in," she cried as soon as the call was answered.

"Yes, I am sure," tears trickled down her face and dropped on the floor.

"Alright," Anika nodded as she felt a nibble in her right toe. It was Mrs. Norris licking her toes as the purring continued.

Staring at the blank space in the wall Anika surveyed through a spider's web. Watching it like a hawk, she observed the struggles of the spider trying to wriggle out of the web. As the door latch opened, Anika twitched. Turning towards the door, she spotted her mother marking her presence.

"You okay?" interrogated the mother, concerned. Anika smiled at a distance, looking at her mother teary eyed.

Holding Mrs. Norris. in her arms, she blurted "I have signed up to be a witness in the court of law." The mother felt a prick in her stomach and the silence continued.

Mind your own butt!

- Shikha Nangru

"Five sachets please" demanded the 30-something lady, tapping her feet as she waited in the queue. Trying to navigate her way through the crowd, Samudrika searched the room left to right supported by the little neck that she had. At last, she found a small table in the corner of the room for doing her job. The lid of the coffee cup was opened by her sausage fingers and the five sugar sachets were poured. With the first sip, several eyebrows caught the stocky woman moaning like a saxophone. Grinning sheepishly at the corner, she decided to move out.

As Samudrika headed home, she picked a pack of jalebis while ordering a plate of butter chicken using her Swiggy. Samudrika did not seem to be in a happy mood though as she opened the locks to her house. No sooner did she open the door than she overheard a conversation going on in the living room. Or was it the television set? She wasn't sure. She kept the pack of Jalebis on the kitchen shelf as she heard her mother.

"How did it go?"

"Just the usual way," Samudrika announced, serving Jalebis to the 50 year old.

"What was it about?" asked the concerned mother as Samudrika turned her back.

"Another funny fat friend with a non-stop eating habit," Samudrika juggled a few peanuts in her mouth.

Opening the crown cap off her Kingfisher Ultra, Samudrika began to settle on the sofa with her mother. As the mother raised her brows questioningly, Samudrika mumbled, "Oh! come on mom. Who said beer is only a man's best friend?"

"So what next?" the poker face switched the channels, landing on an ongoing celebrity interview with anchor and trade analyst Nihar Sinha. The man suited in black continued to smile.

"Samudrika, our viewers would love to know about your role in the film and your overall experience as a part of it."

"It was a great experience Nihar, couldn't have asked for a better role. It was a superb cast," she continued, "I mean can you say it's been a decade almost, right? Everyone still remembers Mithhu Arora and shares memes about the character. It was, indeed, my success story Nihar. The character has grown so popular just like Thakur or Samba in Sholay. It was an instant hit. Mithhu is not just a fat caricature for bringing comic relief, you know. Mitthu brought life to the film."

"Samudrika, why don't you share your experience on the sets of 'Waqt Ki Baatein'?" he requested.

"Well, it was a phenomenal experience on the sets, you know at Blue Parrot Productions they just pamper you to no end. Also, it was such fun with Niharika Khan and Mayank Kapoor on the sets. With such veteran actors in place, of course, I was nervous initially, intimidated too, if I admit. But once we were in it, it was a wholesome and easy experience. In fact, Shaina and I bonded really well as we shot our scenes together, and I'd be happy to say that we're still in touch," Samudrika heard herself say.

Smiling intently, Samudrika continued "You know, I feel so blessed I got the opportunity to work with such a grand production house and so many established actors early on in my career. It was almost a dream come true then, and it's a dream come true now.

Certainly, a defining role in my career. This is not the opportunity that many are bestowed w--"

"Another audition tomorrow," Samudrika switched the channel, rubbing the nape of her neck.

"You should lose some of those extra calories, at least from your butt and your stomach, and your arms, and legs. You know, just saying."

"I'm sorry. When did, you say, you started trading in butt business mom?"

About the author

R.Kaviya *is a senior student in Avinashilingam deemed university, she did her schooling in Vidhya Mandir matriculation school. She was born on 21th November 2001. She always loves to wrap a story and loves to hear one too. She always thought that penning something down will make it permanent, so she started out writing, and put her words on paper. Her passion is to learn something new and to write.*

Connect with her on Instagram:

@kaviyaraaghu11

Rectifying the errors

I was the person who always found fault in others, who hated this life. I always longed for toys, I wasted my food, I skipped many classes. I had a sophisticated life but I never realized the worth of money.

It was a Tuesday night. After dinner, I went to my dad's room. The paralyzed person signaled me to take the diary kept on the table, and asked to read it. But I didn't have time to read it. So I took my essentials and rushed to do my work.

The next day went well. I went home,and asked my mom to cook my favourite *paratha* for me. After finishing it, I did my work, and asked my colleague to finish the remaining work. After my talk with my colleague, I switched the lights off, and went to bed. I was tired, so I fell asleep casily. After some time, when I was fast asleep, I had a nightmare. I was running to grab the dairy but it was running with a great speed. Suddenly, I stopped chasing, the diary. The diary too stopped and appeared like my dad .I was awake and I stepped out from my room. I slowly opened the door of my my dad's room and tiptoed inside. He was asleep. Then I sat besides that dairy and took it in my hand. It was a old-fashioned dairy with a lot of stains on it. I opened the first page. It had a picture of my dad's childhood home. It was a single shed, in which his mom, dad and sister and he used to reside. It had a warm note, scribbled in the form of a poem.

'We all sleep in a common hut,

Where the croaking of frogs is usual.

I ran to school with a skinny body often to satisfy the hunger.

I too have food but it never quenched my thirst,

I don't buy dresses even if they are torn,

I never travelled in a car.

I don't have any toys.

Yes, I cried during Diwali for the revolver toy.

But my dad beat me instead.

There is no strength left in me,,

To cry out loud about poverty.'

My heart chased it's beat. I turned on to the next page. I found the list of monthly groceries.

Bread - 5 packets

Rava -5 packets

Oil - 1 gallon

Vegetable - 100 rupees

With teary eyes, I rushed to the next page. I noticed a picture of dad wearing a black and white outfit, standing in front of some company. Below the picture, a few lines were written:

'I saw poverty in my life. It never let me enjoy any moment. I was poor for half of my life. I was jealous of my friends who ate good food everyday. I decided to give my parents a good life. So I ran for my entire life, as if it was a race. I did many jobs, but the money wasn't enough.

I kept running, working hard. Finally, the day came when I was appointed as an employee with a good pay in a reputed company. I saved my money and now we crossed the monthly limit. The money satisfied our hunger. Days passed and my mother died due to sickness. She often used to say, "When you are hungry, you get confidence to break the hunger, to fill your empty stomach." I rushed and brought money, but I never missed the feel of bringing it. I never brought you anything easily. After you got employed I saw you spent lavishly.

Keep one thing in mind- others might not be getting everything easily, just like you do. That is why you should value everything and spend carefully. If you don't do that, you will end up being poor and you won't be able to buy even the things that you need the most. Always keep in mind that necessities are more important than luxuries.'

I closed the diary as I had learnt the most important lesson in my life.

About the author

Vimal Achintya *is an aspiring writer who so far wrote more than 10 short stories which were featured on various literary magazines and bookstagrams . His works are mostly the thriller types. Each and every story of his ends with a twist that is really a twist and answering all your queries at the end is his another forte.   Go on! You'll be hooked!*

Connect with him on Instagram: @vimal_achintya

The Richfords

"Benjamin Richford, Born: 30- January- 1994. Dead: 10-September 2020".

These words were carved on the gravestone of Ben while he was resting beneath. He was found dead in a fire accident near his house yesterday. Ben was a tough man, aged twenty six. He always wore the same leather coat which his mom had stitched specially for him a year before she died with his father in an accident . The same accident which made him a cripple. Living for more than two years in a wheel chair was his fate till yesterday. Now he would finally rest at ease here.

Ben's funeral took place on 11th of September. His relatives, close buddies, his uncle John who stood by him and his brother Tim after their parents' unforeseen demise, were standing statically as the priest finished off his prayer for Ben's soul. Timothy Richford is Ben's twin brother who now runs the Richford Inc. He and Ben shared a super thick bond. Tim had tried as many ways as possible to make his twin brother stand again. But Ben had failed him by departing soon than he ought to.

Uncle John was an example of a pitch perfect gentleman. His brother Mr. Richford had given him a share in his assets, making him one of the richest persons in his vicinity. People were standing and talking at the funeral ceremony, held at the hall of Ford mansion. John was standing near a casement window watching the rain that was slowly pacing up.

"For Ben" Tim said, firmly handing over a snifter half filled with Adriana.

"For Ben" John said as he borrowed the glass, glancing at people.

"Finally, our plan to eradicate that crippled womb broom was successfully carried out." Tim said in a low but cheerful voice.

"Finally!" John said with smiling face. "How did

you manage to convince Ben to go to the depot?" asked John.

"Simple! I didn't convince him, rather told him that dad and mom's car finally came after long court trail".

"Clever of you!" said John, punching him mockingly.

"And as he was seated inside the car, I hopped out casually and locked it. Then set it on fire." Tim told staring at the window blankly.

"Poor Ben" John said.

"Poor Tim" said Ben looking into John.

"Uncle, you do remember that we are identical twins, right?" John stumbled upon Ben.

"I am terribly guilty for killing my own brother, Uncle. But I had no other way. He had to pay

for what he intended to do to me." said Ben looking at the snifter. There was a moment of silence dwelling.

"Why did you kill my parents Uncle? You were the one driving the car that day voluntarily. I remember you were arguing with my dad about the assets and all of a sudden you accelerated the car whilst turning on a bend. And then I lost consciousness. That's all I can remember."

"After gaining consciousness at the hospital, I heard some saying that I laid down in a pool of blood on the road while our car was burning to

ashes with my parents. Putting the seat belt off had saved my life as mom pushed me out to the road." finished Ben. "That too, I couldn't recall clearly, just assuming".

"Why did you act like a cripple all these years?"

John asked in a voice which seemed like he is

almost fainting.

"Not all the time uncle. I was cured after a year of the accident. I wanted to confront my brother. I knew he'd do this to me. And to make him pay for what he did to our parents".

"How did you know about Tim?" asked John, trembling.

"I'm not that much of a fool, Uncle. The day of the accident was our parents' anniversary. I found it fishy of Tim not showing up with us for celebration. I badly wanted Tim to be a good man. But he ain't one." said Ben seeing John being horrified by what he was hearing.

"He knows something would happen that night but didn't stop us from going. He's your ally, uncle." continued Ben.

Seeing Ben into his eyes, he said in a stammering voice, "You two are not the only identical twins out here Benny".

Ben stumbled on hearing that. His Dad was the only one who'd call him Benny.

"Dad!"

"It was John who died that day son. He did try to escape before crashing our car. But I held him back. I don't know how I survived. I was left at the slope, at the side of the road. I didn't

wanted to turn myself in. I know many people would be out there planning to kill our family, including John. So I decided to hide under his skin so that I can at least save my boys. But once I came to know about Tim, I decided to kill him. So that I can at least save you, Benny. I was about to do the same thing you did to Tim. The salient members of our family had died in this melee, Benny. You're like your mother. Clever lad. You're alive now. Thank almighty for that."

Mr. Richford said, before falling down as a result of the poison.

About the author

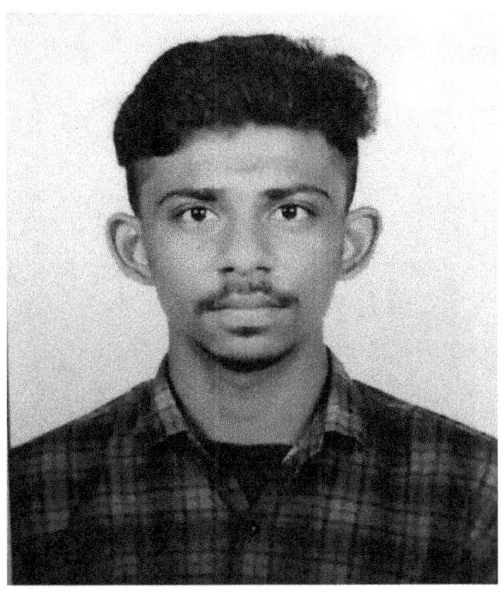

Sanjay Ram *is from Coimbatore, born and brought up in a middle class family filled with happiness. He completed schooling at Coimbatore and is currently pursuing Bachelor's degree in English. He has a greater passion towards writing in both Tamil and English since childhood. He expresses all his thoughts through writing. He has written many of short stories and poems, but he hasn't expressed them out. He thinks he should show his talent to people through his works. He will always love writing and will keep writing more and more. He always writes stories with simple and effective morals, so that people who*

read it will also value small things in their lives. He hopes to bring a smile on their face. That will be the greatest gift he will ever get.

Connect with him on Instagram:

@sanjaydeepakbuggy2327

Live to achieve

The Smith family lived in a small village. There were four members in the Smith family. They weren't too rich, but led a happy and peaceful life . Since the boy, whose name was Joy, was young, his mother used to teach him new things, tell him stories by showing him the beautiful moon.

She used to look after the house and his father used to go to work on the farm. They didn't have many luxuries in life, but they never felt sad about anything. Joy had a younger sister named Bonnie. She was a sweet little girl who used to play with her dolls and she never failed to make people smile and play with her. Both of them were good at studies and used to love to go to school. They always dreamed about achieving great things in life. Even if they were young, they were aware of their family's financial condition. Joy wanted to become an astronaut. Both of them wanted to study and make the most of their lives.

One day, their parents had gone out for some work. They used to travel by their bike, the only vehicle that they ever had. Joy and Bonnie were at home. While returning home, they saw a truck coming in their direction. They thought that the truck will stop and let them go. But the truck didn't stop and kept approaching them. The breaks might have failed. They yelled at the truck driver. They were scared and before they could do anything, everything blacked out. People gathered. There was blood everywhere. Their bike was destroyed badly. The spectators were terrified at the sight. One of them called the ambulance and checked whether both of them are alive or not. Unfortunately, they had passed away on the spot. The ambulance arrived and took their bodies to the hospital. Their friends and relatives were called at the hospital. Some of their family friends picked Joy and Bonnie from home and took them to the hospital. They were feeling sad even after looking at the kids. The kids kept asking them about what had happened, but no one could answer.

Soon, they reached the hospital. They saw their relatives there. The children weren't allowed to go in the morgue room.

But they understood what had happened. They went into a state of deep shock. It took days for Bonnie to understand that her parents are never coming back, no matter how long she waited at the door of their home. Joy was depressed because he had not only lost his parents, but also his support system. His parents meant the world to him. He used to reminisce the memories of the family time that they had spent. He remembered his mother telling him that grandfather is up there, on the moon in that beautiful, dark sky and that they would be on the moon if they weren't with him. He looked up at the sky and saw the moon shining bright in the dark sky and he smiled at the moon. He felt his parents were smiling at him. He smiled with tears in his eyes, promising himself and his late parents that he will become an astronaut and go to the moon. Maybe they'll meet him there.

Years passed. After a lot of sacrifices and struggles, he achieved what he was determined to achieve. He became an astronaut and made his first space travel to moon. He had a great journey to moon and returned back whole wholeheartedly and landed safe on the earth . The day after he returned to earth, he had the most peaceful and happiest night. By that time, Bonnie had also grown up to and had become an engineer. She was working in a multinational company. After Joy had left for his higher studies and work, Bonnie lived with their uncle and aunt.

Bonnie and Joy had become a source of inspiration for everyone. People started telling their kids about how they faced all the difficulties that life threw at him and yet achieved their dreams. Joy was feeling immensely satisfied with himself. He was glad that he and his sister had cone this far in life. His parents had motivated him before and after their death. He could never forget the sacrifices they made for him. They always remained grateful for getting such wonderful parents. But their death was something from which they could never move on completely.

Moral of the story: Anything may happen at anytime in this world. We all are here to fight hard and achieve our dream and goal. Everyone has a purpose in life. Everyone longs for something in their life and tries to achieve it by working hard. Love your parents who had given you life in this world. They are the ones who gave you birth and tried hard to give you the best of everything, every time. Be happy with your parents and love them more than anything in this world.

About the author

Nivetha Chandran *was born in The Nilgiris. She is doing her undergraduate in English literature at Avinashilingam University. She started her writing at lethargy junctures but later she yearned to write. She is very imaginative in her writings. She eternally found nature as her best pal and this made her a creative sage. She desires to tell her readers to "stay optimistic to reach your goal".*

Connect with her on Instagram:

*@_nivethachandran_*

Life of a middle class boy

Once upon a time, a poor man, along with his middle-class family, resided in a small village. He loved his wife Savithiri a lot. They had a late-born child named Munna, who was studying in 9th standard. He was very much interested in and curious about sports, primarily football. He wanted to travel the world to play sports. But due to some financial problems, he couldn't travel anywhere. His focus on education motivated others to do well. Such a good personality he had!

One day, Munna's father had a severe heart attack. Doctors told him that he won't live for more than a week. Munna was concerned about his dad. He was reckoning that hereafter he would take care of his mother because his father was no more healthy to work for his family and his mother was also not good at her health. With wet eyes, he looked into his father's eyes and assured him that he would surely look after his mother. After a week, Munna's father passed away. Now, it was time for Munna to take the responsibility of his mother and their home. He also desired to study and make progress in sports. So he cringed to work in his free time. Every day, in the morning, he went to school and in the evening, he pushed himself to do a part-time job to financially support himself and his mother.

Some days passed. Munna entered the 10th standard. He had a lot to study so he was not able to go to work. For one year, he hesitated going to job and concentrated on his studies. He went to many tournaments and earned a fair amount of money. Finally, he passed 10th standard with the first rank. He got admission for higher studies in sports quota. Munna's mother was very relieved to see his son succeed in whatever he loved and she for cheered him for his hard work. Then Munna continued with his job along with his studies. Belonging to a middle class family had put him through a lot of struggles at a very young age. But all the experiences taught him different things and prepared him for his life.

Later, Munna managed to earn sufficient amount of money to uphold the daily expenses. They shifted from the village to the city. Again he played many football matches and won rewards. These rewards helped him in his higher studies. Munna was delighted that he had fulfilled promised that he had made to his father. He felt satisfied after seeing his mother happy. Him and his mother began dwelling happily.

About the author

Mohanasrrhee K.M *is a new writer in this literary world. This short story is her first attempt. She desires to write anecdotes. Her anecdotes are quite emotional and crazy. She hopes that her anecdote will be interesting and enjoyable, so that the reader keeps perusing them.*

Connect with her on Instagram:

@manchurian_noodles

The proud moment

Once upon a time, there lived a girl called Sara in a small village. She was average in studies and was very eager to do her higher studies abroad. But, she belonged to a middle class family of four members. Yes, of course, the nuclear family. After a few years of living in the village, they decided to move to a town for finding new work. Sara's father had got a new job there. He moved to the town first. He made all the necessary arrangements to live a comfortable life. The house that he rented was small, but felt comfortable. The neighborhood was good and people seemed busy throughout the day. Sara, her mother and her sister were going to move after a few days because they had errands to do. They packed the essential things for taking it to their new house in a town that was once a dream for them. All of them were on cloud nine, as none of them had been to a town even once in their lives, let alone living in one. Sara and her sister were extremely excited to meet new people, go to a new college, participate in different activities and many more exciting things which the town had to offer. But they all were equally scared and tensed as they had always heard that the people living in the town are much different than the villagers. City life is busy and expensive. People wearing stylish clothes, talking in different languages and going out often with their friends or partners is a common scene in any town. They were happy for all the good things that were happening, but anxious about whether they will be able to adapt to the city life or not.

Sara's mother was skilled in various fields like tailoring, embroidery, cooking, arts and crafts and her sister was good in remembering the events that happened before 10 – 15 years. The habit of Sara was to build a kingdom in her mind, a kingdom of her own. She loved to spend time with her sister by clicking funny selfies, imitating each other, chatting for hours, sitting on the terrace and watching people pass by and making fun of the way they walk and talk. Both of them were average in academics, but they were never stressed or depressed because of that. They were aware of the competition among students and job aspirants, but all they could do was to try, to do their best in every situation. Both of them got admitted into a new college in the town. They were in the same college, but in different classrooms, doing different courses. They liked their new college, but they needed some time to get adapt to the college life. Within a few months, they made friends, became familiar with the college, the people and the city. Sara worked as hard as possible to score high. She had made a lot of progress and was gaining confidence. She also began writing poems and short stories, making greeting cards, posters, advertisement, etc. She was truly happy and was loving the city life.

Few days later, Sara came to know that her father was in serious trouble of paying debts. He had taken loans from banks for renting the house, paying Sara's and her sister's college fees, and for settling in the new city. At first, he had thought that he would be able to clear the debt by working overtime and saving more than spending. But it was too much in comparison of his salary. Their needs increased, their lifestyles changed, which had therefore led to the increase in the expenses. As he was the only one who earned money, he was under immense stress. He began to think that the decision of taking up a job in the city was a wrong one.

Her mother was very bold and decided to face the problem. They used to call her 'The Iron Lady of our family.'

"I will start my tailoring work again. It will help us in this hour of crisis and I'll enjoy it too!" she said.

"But are you sure? You look after the household as well. Don't you think it will be stressful for you?" Sara's father was concerned.

"Yes, I am sure. It's just a matter of few days. If I think that it's too much, I'll stop."

"Okay." he said in a low voice.

"We'll get through this together. Everything will be fine." She consoled him.

Meanwhile, Sara was already thinking about saving her money for her higher studies abroad. Her mother was very clear about not allowing her to take up a job before her studies. She eagerly wanted to help her father and her family by earning money. She saved money by walking everyday to college. Her friends used to ask her to go with them to restaurants and cafes, but she used to give some excuse and go home. As she was thinking about earning money, she realized that she can earn money by writing short stories, poems, making greeting cards, posters for events, etc. She participated in a writing competition conducted by her college. She won first prize in poetry. The prize was Rs.5000. She felt good about herself and that at least she had made a start. Her mother didn't know anything about this. As days passed, she wrote many poems and short stories, participated in writing contests, wrote blogs, book reviews, submitted her work to various magazines and earned money through all of these activities. The amount used to be less, but it helped her. After a few months, she decided to count the money that she had saved and earned altogether. She was shocked after counting the money. She couldn't believe herself. She had one lakh rupees! She had never thought that she could do this.

She decided to tell her parents about this. She thought that her mother will get angry on her, but she knew that she had done the right thing for her family. She happily went with the money and handed it over to her father.

"What is this?" he asked.

"Open the bag. I've got something for you, dad." He opens the bag and stared at the amount in shock. "I don't understand. How did you….?"

"I wanted to help you with the debt. So I wrote for magazines, participated in writing contests and won prizes, saved money by walking to college everyday, never went to any restaurant or café with my friends, made greeting cards and sold them. I've been doing this since months and managed to collect one lakh rupees. I didn't tell this to you because I wanted to surprise you...and also because I knew that mom wouldn't allow me to do all this."

Her parents' eyes were filled with tears of happiness. They were extremely happy and felt glad to have a daughter like Sara. That was a proud moment for them.

"Thank you so much dear. I'm sorry you had to go through so much trouble…." Her father said this and hugged her. "I'm really proud of you. I believe that you will do your best in everything."

"I don't think this amount will clear all the debt, but I hope that this will help."

"Yes of course, dear. Thank you for helping me."

She smiled. She felt relieved that she could help her family.

About the author

Dr. Munila Naqvi, an Assistant Professor in a Management College in Lucknow. She has done her PhD in Commerce from University of Lucknow. She was the topper in the merit list of B.Com in the year 2008. A teacher by profession and a writer by passion. She writes prose, poetry and academic books too. One of her book on Higher Education is already published and several other publications in National and International Journals. Dr. Munila Naqvi is involved with various counselling programs and works as a Mentor, at Virtual School for Personality

Development and Professional skills. She has also been involved with delivering invited talks for students' and general public.

Connect with her on Instagram: @drmunilanaqvi

Love on the net

It was a hot summer afternoon, and just like everyday, Shelly logged in her social media account. But she was unaware of the fact, that this afternoon is going to be the changing noon of her life. She suddenly saw some of the notifications appearing on the home screen, and one amongst them was about a new friend request from a "cute boy". She usually deletes the requests from strangers, but this time she felt something different. Shelly went through his profile and kept on staring at his pictures, but did not respond to the request. This continued for few days. She used to visit his profile, see his pictures and then get back to her normal course.

Few days later, she thought that I should befriend this "cute boy". So in the middle of the night, she logged in but to her surprise she did not find that request in the list anymore. Shelly got anxious and could not understand what she is feeling and why. That night she could not slept properly, and as soon as she woke up the next morning, she started searching for him on the social media. And finally her efforts turned out successful as she was able to find that guy. She immediately sent him a request, along with a long message.

"I don't know why I didn't add you in my friend list, but I had been seeing your profile for the past few days without your knowledge and peeping into your whereabouts, likes, dislikes, personal pictures.....so I am extremely sorry for that".

Before that message could reach the "cute boy", he accepted her request. And to her message he replied "I am honored, that you spent your time to message me".

Shelly could not gather courage to utter a word or write something. She was completely lost in the thoughts that it is a sarcasm or a compliment ?

Days passed. She always visited his profile and checked everything about him, but did not find courage to talk to him. But she always held it in her heart, that may be someday he texts me and asks me how I am ?

So finally her dream came true. After 6 months of being friends, this was the first time, he texted her saying "Hey Shelly, this is your cute boy Neil" . She had just logged in, but till now she had lost all hopes that they will ever talk. But destiny had different plans. The moment she saw the notification, she could not control her excitement. Seeing his message, and finally getting to know his name "Neil", she repeated it many times in different tones "Neil, Neeeiil, Neeiiilll". Shelly just couldn't get out of that line "Your cute boy" as if she has started considering him as her lover.

They never looked back from that day. They were so much engrossed in chats, without realizing the time and hours they were spending on it. For them, there was nothing more beautiful and exciting than talking to each other and knowing every little detail about each other.

One day in a random conversation, he said "It's almost 5 months since we are talking to each other. So I guess this is the right time to say this. Shelly, I want to hold on to you forever."

She got confused with the statement and said "What....what?".

He said "I want to marry you".

Shelly could not control her tears, because for her it was love at first sight, that she never expressed. But it was like as a dream come true. The very same evening Neil called her on the chat messenger. It was the first time that they were hearing each others' voices.

She got anxious seeing his name appearing on the screen "Cute Boy" and with every ring her heart started to beat faster. Finally, she answered the call and the cute boy uttered "Hey Shelly, I am still waiting for your answer. Be it Yes or No, I will not question you in any way. But do let me know."

She took a deep breath and said, "I had fallen in love with you the day I saw your display picture on your social media account. After saying this, she kept silent and said, "I always wanted to be with you."

Hearing this over the phone, Neil started dancing in joy. The emotions started emerging happiness, excitements, joy and tears all at the same time. And before hanging up the call, Neil said, "Text me your number."

Shelly got confused. She thought that is he going to ask for some close picture, or what ? Her tone fumbled and she said, "What is it Neil? Speak up."

He said, "I love you". Her anger vanished and in a blink of a moment she burst into giggles and tears.

This was the new beginning of a new life for Neil and Shelly. It was their beautiful love story that blossomed on the Internet. So, finally the chats, and telephonic conversations took a back seat and they decided to meet in person and the 17th of March, was finalized.

They both had already started living in their virtual home, where both of them treated each other as a couple. Every day began with the plans for future, and ended with working on them. So at last, it was time to convert their dream into reality. It was decided between them, that immediately after meeting, Shelly will take Neil to her parents and he will express his wish to marry, because Neil had already cleared from his side that he will marry the girl of his choice, and his parents had given their consent.

Shelly was sure enough that there wasn't a single reason to reject Neil. He was good looking, had good family background and decent job profile. But deep down, she was really scared about his parents disapproving of her. She promised herself that no matter what, she will fight for her love.

The meeting time was fixed at 12:00 P.M in the afternoon, at "Love birds cafe". They spent the night in sleeplessness, thinking about each other and imagining a world of happiness. So, finally the 17th of March arrived, she could not decide what to wear red, pink or yellow. After the confusion for almost an hour, she finalized a red top, with blue jeans, keeping her hairs untied, with earrings and bangles on. She kept on standing before the mirror for hours trying to see herself in every manner. So that she looks perfect before Neil.

On the other hand, Neil was equally excited with the thought of seeing his Shelly for the first time. An ocean of emotions were emerging, but he kept himself calm. So they both stepped out to see each other. Shelly booked a cab to reach to her love, and Neil took his bike. And finally the most awaited moment arrived. They were on the opposite sides of the road, badly stuck in a jam. So immediately Shelly called Neil and said, "What should I do? I am stuck on the crossroad. He asked her to come out of the cab and walk towards the cafe.

The moment she stepped out, he was standing on the other side of the road, and he had a first glance of Shelly, his heart skipped a beat. He put his helmet down and started waving to her with broad smile.

The smile was so enchanting that she got lost in it, without realizing where she is. Shelly started taking faster steps to reach soonest to Neil, but destiny had different plans for them. Before they could celebrate their love and could actually hug each other, a speeding SUV hit Shelly from the back. Neil was shocked. He could not do anything except for crying. He ran towards her. She was profusely bleeding. The car driver was caught and taken to the police station, and Shelly was taken to the hospital. But the doctors could not save her. Neil was completely shattered. Their dream of living together came to an end. Their love story just stayed as "Love on the Net" and nothing beyond that. He went close to Shelly, and kissed on her forehead with teary eyes and said, "Your cute boy will always love you Shelly".

Poles apart

- Dr. Munila Naqvi

Marriage was not on the cards for Piya, a 27 years old young, vivacious, enthusiastic woman, belonging to an upper middle class family, who believed in self dependence and living life on her own terms. She had completed Masters in Business Administration, and working as an Assistant Manager with a top brand. She was highly contented with her life and enjoying every bit of it. But her family was consistent with the same thing i.e "to get her married, as its already too late". This was the daily dining table discussion at the Malhotra's house. But every time, she convinced them with her clever tricks.

But life took a round turn when her father, Alok Malhotra, met with an accident and was partially paralyzed. They consulted the best of the doctors, but there wasn't any ray of hope. This was a traumatic time for the entire family, but Piya and her mother Sarita tried their best to keep him motivated.

Time passed by, but there wasn't a slight change in his condition, rather some more names of medicines were added to the list. It was a winter evening, when all three of them were having a hot cup of Coffee. All of a sudden Mr. Malhotra said, "I am not sure for how long I am going to live, but I only wish to see Piya getting settled in life."

The situation was so tough, that in spite of trying to refuse, she just nodded her head and said, "Yes, as you wish. I am ready for getting married. Saying this, she ran upstairs. This was the moment for her parents that they were eagerly waiting for.

From the very next day, the atmosphere at Malhotra's house became joyous, and days and nights were spent in discussing about boys for Piya. After rigorous hardwork for 2 months, her parents decided upon a boy who works with a bank as a Manager, and lives just 15 kilometers away from their place. So, finally after all hustle bustle, a meeting was decided, where the boy, named Ansh, and his family came to see Piya.

Piya's parents were so excited, as they believed its just going to be the D-day for her. She just kept herself calm and decked up beautifully in green salwar suit to meet Ansh and his parents. When the Malhotras met Aroras, they were equally happy to find the family equal in status, and every other thing. So both the parents consented for the relationship. But now the final decision lied with the boy and the girl.

So their parents asked them to talk in private and came up with a positive response. They both headed towards the garden. They sat there. Piya gathered courage to tell him the truth. So after 10 minutes of pin drop silence, she spoke up loudly "I don't want to marry, so please could you say no?"

Ansh was shocked to hear this. It appeared to him that she just poured out her heart. He burst into laughter, and said, "I was about to say the same thing to you. But to my surprise, you said it." They both laughed loudly, that how destiny made them meet. So they asked each other the reason for not marrying, Piya shared her whole story.

Then she asked the same to Ansh. He said, "I love a girl named Ran., But my parents have disapproved her because she is lower in status and family family background."

She interrupted in between, "You should have taken a stand if you love someone."

Ansh's eyes turned moist and he said, "I tried, but my parents threatened me that if I marry her, I will have to end all relations with them. It was a tough choice for me. Leaving her broke my heart." This made Piya sad.

"But you can help me? He asked.

"How can I help you?"

"Let's get married, but with a pact."

"A Pact?

"Yes, an agreement that we will stay as friends and after 6 months you will give me a divorce. then I can easily marry Rani. And in your case, your parents' wish will also be fulfilled. You will get married, and that marriage will fail. Then you can live as you want. She liked the idea and they shook hands and said "Done".

They both went back home after half an hour. Parents were eagerly waiting for them to announce their decision. They smiled at each other, and said "Yes, we like each other." The Malhotra's house turned into celebratory zone, laughter, giggles, hugs and smiles all on sparkled the floor.

The preparations for the big day began from buying exquisite furniture, to accessories, apparels and booking grandeur lawns and making appointments with top boutiques and parlors. The Malhotra house was filled with joy, and relatives had started making random visits, discussing the dos and dont's during her wedding.

Finally, after all the excitement, Piya got married to Ansh. The moment for which her parents waited for so long, had finally came. Their eyes were filled with tears of joy and pride. For, they had found such a suitable match for her.

Amidst all this, they both were equally nervous thinking about how life is going to be for them. She reached Arora's house, as a daughter in law. A huge number of relatives were waiting to welcome her, with a number of rituals to be performed. Piya was not at all interested in all this, but she was left with no other option except being a part of it. Finally, the rituals ended at 3:00 A.M. She took a sigh of relief.

They were taken to a beautifully decked room, decorated with candles and flowers with beautiful fragrances. Seeing all this, she felt a chill going down her spine.

She just looked at him and said " Our marriage is just for the name sake, and you love someone else. Have you forgotten all that?"

"Calm down. I remember each and everything but I can't disclose it to my parents. They have played their part and we are going to do as we have decided.

She smiled and said "I must say, you are a real gentleman." He smiled back too.

Months passed by, and their marriage was turned into a strong friendship. They started valuing each other and they never failed to make each other happy by doing small gestures. Once, Ansh was going to be late in returning home. He informed his mother but didn't called Piya. Because he knew that's its just friendship. Piya kept on watching the time and started panicking as it was too late for him to return. Without giving it a thought, she called Ansh, and worriedly asked "Where are you? Its too late."

He was surprised to see her asking so worriedly. He took a pause and said, "This isn't the first time that I'll be coming home late. But are you okay?

Piya said nothing and asked the same question to herself. *'Where am i going? I know we are into this relationship for a temporary period and he loves somebody else.'*

She finally gathered herself and promised herself not to behave like a wife because its just an agreement that will end one day.

Likewise, an entire year passed by, and they were happily enjoying each other's company. And the girl that Ansh loved, had got married to another guy and moved abroad. Ansh has almost forgotten her, and his life revolved around Piya and his parents.

But one day, his mother asked Ansh, "I feel there is something that you are hiding."

He denied it completely. But after a few minutes, he broke down before his mother. And with moist eyes, narrated the whole story. His mother could not control her tears.

She said, "Its wrong of you to do this. You have played with my sentiments."

He apologized and pleaded guilty for his act, but his mother said its enough now. If that girl considers it as an agreement, lets end it. I am going to call her parents tomorrow to end this drama. Before he could say anything, she went to her room.

Ansh was sinking, he didn't know how to react and what to explain to Piya. On the other hand, Piya had started realizing that she has developed feelings for him. So she decided to speak her heart out to him. After the dinner, Ansh asked Piya to come to the terrace. She started feeling that he too feels the same for her and is going to confess. She changed her attire, combed her hair and put up a light make up, as if she is going on a midnight date with Ansh. She kept herself calm, but deep inside she was dancing with joy. She reached the terrace where Ansh was already sitting, staring at the stars. This appeared really romantic to her. She walked slowly towards him, and said "See, I am here."

Ansh was stunned by her pretty looks. She never appeared this beautiful to him. He held his breath and said, "I need to tell you something really important."

She asked excitedly "What is it?"

He looked into her eyes, and said "Tomorrow your parents are coming."

"Oh wow!" Piya got excited on hearing this. But her excitement couldn't last for long.

When Ansh completed his sentence "...to take you with them." She still didn't understand. Then he said, "Now, no more pretending. Tomorrow everything is going to end."

She was shocked to hear this, but managed to control her emotions.

Ansh said "My mother knows everything about it and she says that a marriage, if treated as an agreement, is meaningless. So better to end it, and free yourself and Piya from this unwanted bond."

They both were shattered deeply, but did not find enough words to tell each other, that they want to stay together. Though things started on a bitter note, everything went good. They kept on looking at each other with thousands of unsaid words.

Ansh said, "Go and enjoy the last night here, because from tomorrow you will be at your place and in your room." Tears started rolling down her cheeks, she left the terrace without uttering a word.

The next morning Mr. Arora, called the Mr. Malhotra and shared with them the whole dramatized marriage. They were in a state of shock. They couldn't believe how their daughter can be so selfish and could play a game in the name of marriage. Mr. Arora talked to their lawyer, and divorce papers were ready.

In the evening, the entire family gathered, to mark the end of this marriage pact. Piya could not gather courage to face her parents. Aroras and Malhotras sat around the table with the lawyer, and it was decided that they both will sign on the divorce paper and then both will be free to live as they want. Ansh was completely lost in all good times he had with Piya, and Piya too started recollecting the memories of smiles and happiness with him. They didn't want to end this relationship, but didn't understand how to explain this to their parents, because they were feeling cheated and betrayed by their children.

The lawyer broke the silence, that was there for over an hour. And said these are the papers, sign it. He kept the papers before Piya. She just looked at Ansh as if asking him to stop her from signing the divorce papers.

She could not control herself, and burst out loudly. "I can't imagine my life without him. I don't know how, when and where I fell in love with him. I apologize to each one of you for hurting your sentiments. It was my immaturity to think of marriage as an agreement. I disrespected the institution of marriage and I am regretting it badly. Hearing all this, Ansh too stood up with teary eyes.

"We made a mistake, and we are sorry for that. You have full right to punish us in any way, but please let us be together. For the past one year, life to me means Piya. We didn't realize earlier but now we know it strongly that we are meant for each other."

Aroras and Malhotras hugged each other, and the celebrations began once again, but this time for a real reason. Ansh and Piya had understood it clearly, that no matter how different two persons are, the only thing that makes them one is love.

About the author

Shikha Patel *lives in Qatar with her partner. She is an urban planner by profession, but she also writes short stories and poetry. She actively blogs in her free time these days. She loves addressing narrative of human experiences. She finds inspiration by observing nature and people and strongly believes to treat them both right! She believes that words have the power to change the destined.*

Connect with her on Instagram:

@_shikha_patel_author_poet

(not enough) Words

It doesn't matter how much you think you love a person; it always feels "not enough", compared to how you feel when you are loved. I share the same kind of skewed relationship with my daughter. I have truly loved her since the day she came into our lives. But being brought up in the Indian society, I was never able to be her best friend. I was shy and uncomfortable confessing to her that I care about her the most. It was easier when her mother was alive. She spoke for me. She expressed for me. All I had to do after that was give a loving glance to my daughter. I managed that swimmingly. Then my wife left us both in a very awkward situation when she just decided to give up on life. I blame her. She should have fought cancer harder. My daughter was 16 and I was 44; we stopped expressing.

Days passed by. I was busy with my job and she was busy making a career. There were nights when she came to me to seek advice regarding what major she should choose in college. We would discuss for hours and I felt proud. *'My daughter believes in me. She discusses her career choices with me. She thinks high of me.'*, were my thoughts at those times. She used to share her achievements and we had our bonding days, when we used to order pizza and watch old movies. Oh! We cannot watch new movies or movies we hadn't seen earlier. I didn't know how to watch an intimate movie scene with my daughter. We, Indian men are not brought up to even think of it. Though I didn't approve of the stereotypical men in my country, I was very much one of them. Yes, hypocrite me!

My daughter turned 22 and on the dinner table one night, she told me she likes this guy from work. I felt like someone hit a hammer past my heart. I knew this would happen one day, but never expected it so soon. I met the guy and of course, I didn't like him. I explained to my daughter that he is not the right guy, and she could do much better. The truth was, no guy was good enough for my daughter. Period. My daughter kept dating him. My heart melted when she came home crying one day and said "Its over". Honestly, I couldn't take her crying but I was relieved. I couldn't process my little girl having another man in her life.

Few years later, I introduced her to my best friend's son. They hit it off and got married. I cried. I cried a lot that night. I regretted not hugging her enough, not kissing her enough, not holding her hand enough. I wanted to do it all again. I wanted to redo it right, not the way I was trained to do it. It took me few months but I came out of the grief. I got a life of my own. My job, evening walks with my friends, weekly poker meet up and daily Netflix-ing kept me occupied. Every Sunday, my daughter used to call me religiously. We talked, but we hardly could talk. She used to tell me about her trips, her job and what new recipe she learnt. She was always happy. I am not sure if she genuinely was happy or she thought I was not capable of understanding her problems. I could never blame her. I did not talk with her either.

Today, I miss her a lot. I planned to clean her room and re-arrange her things. I want to spend a day with her. On her study table, I found her old diaries. They must have been written after her mother died. I battled in my head if I should read it. I wasn't sure if

I was strong enough to read it. However, I managed to take one to my study and opened the first page of her largest diary, titled – "Unsaid words to my father".

About the author

Divit Lokesh Perumalla is good at writing a story in a simple but connecting way. He's also good at fiction& fan fiction, suspense, drama and thriller. He is an author for self help books . You can find the real you with his narrative story, poem and quotes. He always says ‘**it's all in the mind!!**’

Connect with him on Instagram:

@lokee_meansalot_025

With pleasure
(broken hearts & blended hormones)

"Welcome to the hostel life in Dr. Jee Medical & IIT academy(separate hostel for boys & girls). Now Let's go ma'am we'll check our hostel room. Come on Eesha (Eesha Agarwal)follow me." Hostel warden (Sandeep Singh) took them to the hostel after the admission process and gave them the room key of their selection. .

"In each room 2 girls and no class for today."

"Ma'am, but classes will start from Monday." He said while leaving.

"Sandeep sir please send someone in my room. I can't sleep alone at new a place." said Eesha

"Yes sir! But send someone who is good at studies."

"Okay Eeshu! Call me in the evening. Take care of yourself. Bye dear!", said Eesha's mother. Both dispersed by waving at each other.

As he said, by the evening, a new girl names Rebba Agarwal came to share the room with her. Both became good friends in no time. And they went downstairs to call Eesha's mother. On the same day, two boys named Rahul Khanna and Karthik Ayyangar also joined the academy. Same time, same room, in the same way they both shared.

Now the magic begins ...

From Monday everyone began attending the classes, getting involved in their studies and engaged with the curriculum.

One week passed away. They used to chat for the whole day and if they didn't feel sleepy at night, they used to stay up.

Their conversations used to be like....

Eesha: "Darling, Ms. Agarwal! Have you ever been in love with someone?", she winked.

Agarwal: "Nah. I haven't met the ideal guy... the guy with all the ideal qualities which I want in him...", she replied with a sad face.

Eesha: "Ah, I see. No worries, dear. You will definitely find a beautiful....."

Agarwal: "Huh? What?"

Eesha: " Sorry! I mean, you will find the most handsome...."

Eesha: "I don't have in mind any special qualities to look in a guy. I just want someone who is romantic and who will make out for long hours, that too passionately."

Agarwal: "Ooh! So what will you do on the first night after getting married?" she teased.

Eesha gave a romantic expression. She drew her hands onto Rebba Agarwal's thighs and said, "You have such tough and stylish thighs. Smooth and tempting thighs, you have. But these thighs belong to me this night." and she started kissing Agarwal's lap all over around.

Meanwhile, Rebba Agarwal closed her eyes for a moment, as if she was enjoying the moment. But all of a sudden, she opened her eyes and stopped Eesha.

"What's wrong with you, Eesha? What are you doing?"

From the moment after that incident, she stopped talking to Eesha. And Eesha was completely mad about Rebba's beauty and crazy about her attractive outline curves, and deep down, had feelings for her intimating skin tone and facial glow.

Another week passed by.

Rebba had fallen in love with Rahul Khanna and Rahul started feeling the same for Rebba in a very short time. But they never confessed to each other. The magic still continues.

Another weekend comes up.

Eesha got a chance to please Rebba. Somehow Eesha managed to convince Rebba and apologize for her behaviour and requested her to be her friend, just a normal friend. Finally both the Agarwals reunited. But Rebba warned Eesha to take care about behaving nicely next time.

Rebba: "It's a shame to be like that, being a child born in Agarwal family, Eesha. I'm talking to you. Where are you looking at?"

Eesha sits up straight and starts telling her story. "My father Late.Mr. Deepak Agarwal was the Colonel of The Indian Army, and my lovely mother was a mathematics teacher for the 12th grade. We used to meet my father once in a year, that too only for a month. The only thing that we were unhappy about was that he used to always doubt my mother about having affairs with other men while he was away. They used to quarrel a lot. But I was the one who could see his love for me. To be honest, one day, I saw my mother kissing the girl who used to come for the tuition at our home. That was completely shocking for me since I was a school going girl and I didn't know the reason behind what was going on and what she was going through. But after growing up and gaining a little maturity, I realized that I was attracted towards girls not boys. May be I was convinced by my mother about how men treat women like they're nobodies. And I was really running a misconception in my mind about marital life. I'm really sorry, darling...Oh! Sorry! I'm sorry.."

Rebba: "No issue Eesha. You can call me 'darling'. I don't mind, okay? We're like family, #Theagarwalspride.

Eesha: "Well! I don't know how my hormones are different and I'm truly love you. The most for your body and just look at you...,How beautiful you are! I've never seen such a beautiful girl in my entire life. I'm unable to control my feelings for you . Your sparkling smile. And your pretty, smooth and pleasant smelling, wavy hair. You can even become Miss India!" she paused. "Oh, I'm sorry. I shouldn't have said that." Rebba completely understood her situation and started treating her as her best friend.

Rebba: "Don't worry dear. From today, I'm here to make you feel normal and if you do the next time also, I will not kill your feelings. All I wanted is to make you feel normal to save the pride for Agarwal's family.

From now onwards, you've to follow my guidelines. If you follow them, I can cooperate with your feelings once a week. And I request you to try for a week at least otherwise it will hurt me and my efforts will go waste. Okay? Please keep living your normal life and save the pride of the Agarwal family.

After listening to her words, Eesha's eyes opened and glowed with a spark. "Love you so much darling. I had never expected that you'd say this. But I'm really happy to know that you understand me."

Now the real music starts playing....

Both started concentrating on their studies with a new energy and they competed with themselves. They had potential and therefore they managed to score good marks in every subject.

So everyday Rebba taught her about how girls feel when they see a boy and vice versa. She used to exaggerate everything about boys' fantasy. Just like that, she talked about how a girl feels about boys, how does she dreams about boys, how does she admires boys, how does she pays attention to boys, how does she grabs attention of boys and so on.

Here's the triggering point. Eesha was very good at development the entire week. So now it was time for the madness to unwrap.

Let's see the madness of Eesha for her.

Eesha: "Baby! Just wear a T-shit and shorts and nothing inside.

Rebba: "Eesha! This is too much! You're being too bold!"

Eesha: "I don't mind, darling. You strive for Agarwal's pride. I strive for my pleasure ,WITH PLEASURE."

This is all we know.

Rebba: "Then I can't do this anymore. I'm trying to change you, but I might change instead. I'm   disgusted at your f*cking dilection. Holy shit! F*cking crap!"

Eesha: "Baby! Please don't say that. Don't you see my love for you. Anyways, if this is your final decision, then I have a trailer for you. Please do watch this!" Eesha showed Rebba the video that she captured while she was kissing her.

Agarwal: "You lustre! All I was trying to do is to help you, to think for your own good. But how lustful you are!"

Eesha: "All I did was for that moment, and it was not intentional. I was at my peak weak moment, darling. I didn't do anything wrong. Only for pleasure and WITH PLEASURE! I wished that you will understand."

Rebba: "I don't think it's love. It's creepy f*cking lust! How could you do this to me? I tried to do the best for you and you are being the worst with me!?"

Eesha: "Why don't you understand my feelings for you ? Anyway you've no way to outrun me."

Agarwal: "Oh really! If that's the case, every girl in the class will no longer be our friend. You'll miss me as a friend and you miss all the girls in our class. This is how you're gonna end up. Such a thing should happen with you because you deserve it!"

Eesha: "Please darling. I will obey you, whatever you say. But please don't leave me alone and don't even avoid me, ever. I will not be able to take it. Now what's the best that I can do?"

Agarwal: "Let's make a fair deal. All I wanted was to keep you away from myself. Please stay away from me. Please don't touch me anymore, please!"

Eesha: (After thinking for a while) Okay! But can I get a chance? Just one?"

Rebba: "Okay! But one and only one." *'Somehow I should manage to skip this lesbian drama, otherwise I would fall into a trap and who knows I might even change and become like her.'* Rebba was thinking about making a plan for her diversion.

Eesha: "I want you if I get you down in the mark list below my name, as names are listed based on the ranking."

Rebba: "That's impossible. Sounds like a challenge. I agree, but only you should win over me with genuine marks, and the ball will be in my court now."

Eesha: "Let the ball hit the goal this time and I will score the goal. Watch me!"

Rebba started thinking, waiting for a chance to steal her phone and delete the video, so that there will be no threat anymore. When Eesha went for a bath, Rebba took Eesha's mobile and tried to unlock but the password was changed. She failed all the attempts. Eesha wore her bathrobe, came out of the bathroom and saw her.

Eesha: "Darling! Is everything okay with you? You look dull and unwell."

Rebba: "No. I'm alright. Thanks. You just dress up and I'll be just back in a moment."

Rebba left the room and walked in the corridors thinking about something that should be done to get out of the burning kiln. Eesha was standing behind the door and eyeing how she was pacing in the corridor.

The same thing was running parallel behind the scenes with Rahul Khanna and Karthik Ayyangar. This time, Karthik Ayyangar was watching from behind the door.

Days and months passed. After a few months, something bad happened. Rebba and Rahul didn't even know each other until they planned something. The biggest thunderstorm happened. Rebba made an arrangement in the room with all the planning to intoxicate Eesha with the intimacy. Rahul got some beer to make Ayyangar high.

Now let's see how the parallel romantic drama followed....

After many trials, one day looked close for them. This time, Eesha and Ayyangar took the chance.The real tragedy happened was both Rebba Agarwal and Rahul Khanna ended their love, even without a proposal. Rahul got a video that was completely nude & bold, smooching & licking all over the body with Eesha and Rebba. Same way Rebba got a video which was showing intimate relations between Rahul and Ayyangar. In no time, Eesha and Ayyangar with a teamwork made their plan successful. Both the cute lovers (Rebba Agarwal & Rahul Khanna) ended up as mute lovers. They split-separate with Eesha and Ayyangar.(Rebba with Eesha & Rahul with Ayyangar) Then the romantic music ended up in a deep silence. The heavily broken hearts (Eesha & Ayyangar), daily WhatsApp status, Instagram stories filled their broken Everest love and melted the glacier bond with Rahul and Rebba. They flipped their hormones.

Meanwhile Broken Hearts & Blended Hormones made Eesha and Ayyangar fall for each other, understanding each other's pain. The real effort made by Rebba Agarwal and Rahul Khanna worked for now. The real love of Eesha & Ayyangar for Rebba & Rahul melted their emotions convinced their mind.

....Eesha Agarwal weds Karthik Ayyangar....

This time Rebba Agarwal and Rahul Khanna ended up broken with a WhatsApp status.

Love has no limits and limitations. It happens with anyone, without anything but just in a moment. One should never insult someone's love, irrespective of their gender. You're no more eligible for love otherwise.It's constitution!

Our new couple started updating Instagram story .....

'We fell in Love .... We felt the Love ... We're in fellowship with Love!'

About the author

Radhakrishnan Santhose Kumar *is a 15-year old boy, born in Rajapalayam, India. He grew up in Singapore. Writing to him is about something that can help him to relieve stress or which helps him to explore his creativity. He got into writing because he is interested in rapping. He's been rapping since 12 and started writing poems as the lyrics of his rap, as it is all about poetry and rhythm.*

Connect with him on Instagram: @santhose123

When the time comes...

Who is it about: A poor boy named Kumar, aged 15-year and his younger brother Karthi is 11 year old.

Where is the setting: A classic setting of a slum.

What is it about: A boy who wants to pursue his dream of becoming a musician.

Family background: Father is a heart patient and is unable to do any work. Mother works as a construction worker.

What they always do : They are just normal local people. Both of the boys Karthi and Kumar picks up charcoal from train tracks to get pocket money . They always cross the train track to go to school and a train station is just nearby where they cross. They work at a tea stall to help their father with his medical treatment.

One day they saw an advertisement on television at the tea stall, attracting people to participate in a competition and the winner gets a money of 3 lacks. Which is the exact amount needed for their father's medical treatment. They wanted to participate in the competition but they had no experience in music and singing and for participating in the competition, they would need to go to a faraway city for the audition.

They both were spending time thinking of what they could do next, at the train station. There was a person sitting beside them at the train platform watching a YouTube video where a person raps and another person beatbox. They started a conversation with the stranger. The stranger was waiting for his train which seemed to be taking a while to arrive. So both the brothers asked what they were doing and the stranger told them what the people in the video were doing. He told them that they were beat-boxing and rapping. The brothers were very interested in doing it, but they didn't know the song as it was in a different language and they didn't know how to beatbox. The brothers asked how to beatbox. The stranger was a beatboxer, so he taught them some basic sounds and they learnt it quickly. The stranger told them to practice regularly to make it perfect. The train arrived and the stranger boarded the train.

The brothers were walking back home beatboxing so that they could make it perfect and to make sure they won't forget it. They spent days practicing. They even practiced at the tea stall. They eventually realized someone has to rap a song for them, but they didn't know any rap songs as they didn't have a mobile or a television at home. So they eventually decided to write their own rap song about life. They spent time getting the song to go on smoothly

Their father was suffering so much and he didn't want his family to suffer and spend money on his medical treatment, as it could be used for their meal and other needs. They saved a bit of their money on travel to go to the audition and they bought some costumes as they were going to be on television. Their parents didn't know about his. They felt that the journey will be risky as they have never been to that city and didn't know anyone living there. They felt it might be a waste of time if they lose the competition.

On the audition day, they skipped school and took a bus to go to the city. After reaching there, they were nervous but they had the determination so they went for registration, which is a procedure that needs to be done before going to the audition. So they both went to the registration booth. The staff asked them to write their name and stuff. Finally, they were asked for parents signature but they didn't bring their parents along. So they didn't know what to do. One of the brothers asked if it is compulsory to bring their parents. The staff member said yes. Instead of saying they were not accompanied by an adult, they said that they are with an adult and went off saying that their house is nearby and that they will bring a parent. But they started asking strangers for help no one came up to help them. So they asked a beggar, but the beggar accepted the deal only after they give him a certain amount of money.The beggar wrote the name of the brothers' father and they got into the audition somehow and waited in the queue for a very long time. Finally, it was their turn and they were called in.

Kumar started rapping and his younger brother Karthi was beatboxing the judges were really surprised by listening to the rap. They loved it. Kumar and Karthi got accepted and felt very happy and went back home right in time. When their mother asked the brothers for the money, which was earned by working at the tea stall, they told her that they went out to play so they didn't go to work.

One day,they wanted to buy a shirt for themselves at a street. While walking on the street, they saw a music stall newly open. They got interested in learning musical instruments so they decided to checked out the music stall. But they got kicked out because they looked poor, with torn slippers and messy hair with a very local accent and they felt very bad and thought of how the society is against them.

They wanted to give up. But they were still determined to win the competition and help their father. They skipped school, went for the auditions and were winning every round and finally they went to a danger zone and somehow overcame it.

The mother somehow knew that they went for competition as she saw a stranger watching a video of the both brothers performing and she got shocked in seeing their kids performing. The mother went home after work and asked them about whatever was going on .They had no idea of how she knew and they had no choice but to admit the truth. When she asked about why they went for the competition, they told her that they will get 3 lakhs if they win the competition, which it could be used for father's treatment. The mother felt so proud of them. She supported them for their passion.

They went for their semi-finals. They won it and secured a position among the top 5 contestants.They were delighted and had the confidence since the beginning that they will win the competition and help their father. They went back home happily to tell their mom that they have won their semi finals .The father's condition had worsened and they had no choice other than admitting them to a government hospital. They worked hard and at their finals, they did exceptionally well. They were the title winners! They got the cheque of 3 lakhs and gave a speech. They were extremely happy and proud of their success. People applauded them. They went back to the hospital with the cheque. They were tensed about their father's condition. At the hospital, their mom was crying while standing beside the dead body of their father. The brothers were deeply shocked. They started crying with the mother. Their father's funeral was carried out by them, with heavy hearts and teary eyes.

As they had won the competition, they were asked to give speeches and interviews at different places. In all their speeches, they didn't forget to mention their father and pay respect to him.

Other anthologies compiled and published by Shreya Pataskar:

- Voices of the Heart: a collection of wonderful poems

- The Unforgettable Stories: a collection of remarkable short stories

- The Miscellany of Odes